D1480231

Twinkle, Twinkle Mommy Star

Written by
Judith Newell

Illustrated by
Paul Howell

Boyle
&
Dalton

Book Design & Production
Columbus Publishing Lab
www.ColumbusPublishingLab.com

Copyright © 2015 by Judith Newell
LCCN 2015943386

All rights reserved. This book, or parts thereof, may not be reproduced in any form without permission.

Print ISBN 978-1-63337-048-7
E-book ISBN 978-1-63337-049-4

Printed in the United States of America
1 3 5 7 9 10 8 6 4 2

Whatever you put in your heart will stay there forever.

Hope lives on forever even though we do not.

To all of our little ones that have lost someone they love

When I look at the stars, I wonder if my Mommy is somewhere up there with them. I wonder where she lives now. I wonder if she can see me from Heaven. I wonder if that big star in the sky is really her shining down on me. I think I will call it the Mother Star.

I ask my MeMe, "Does Mommy live beyond the stars now? How does she stay up there without falling to earth? Does she have wings? Can she still see me? Is she with our dog, Jazzy? Is she with anyone she knows?"

"She is in Heaven, Peyton," MeMe tells me. "She is taking care of your dog, Jazzy, and she is among people who love her, just like she was here on Earth."

That makes me feel better. But I still miss her so much. Sometimes I feel so sad I don't feel like playing. I feel like I just want to cry.

Daddy says it's OK to cry.

"Tears can wash away the hurt in our hearts, Peyton," he says.

That makes me feel better. So I cry.

At school, I watch the other kids play. I wonder if they know how lucky they are to still have their mommies.

My best friend, Jacob, still has his mommy, and his daddy. They have a big family with lots of brothers and sisters to play with. I like going to his house after school. His family is nice to me. If I'm feeling really sad, they all cheer me up.

Mommy always liked to be around her friends too. She had lots of friends, and she loved having them over to our house. Our house is not as full of people now like it used to be, but Daddy does a good job letting me have lots of my friends over to play.

I worry about what will happen to Daddy and me without Mommy.

One of my friends told me to have Daddy go to the mall, because that's where all the women are. He could pick out a new mommy for us. She would be a "stepmom," which aren't your real mommy, but they are still fun, my friend said.

I ask MeMe if she thinks Daddy should go to the mall.

"Peyton, it's not as easy as that," she says. "But don't worry. Trust your Daddy and when the time is right, someone special will come into your lives."

That makes me feel better. I believe that someday we will be all right again.

As time goes by, I feel less sad. Rainy days make me feel better too. Some kids don't like it when it rains because it means they can't play outside. I like it when it rains because it's like little pieces of Heaven coming down to Earth. The rain makes me feel like Mommy is still here with me.

"Peyton, she is always just one room away," MeMe tells me.

Sometimes at night I like to lay in bed and say the word "mother" over and over. "Mother." I just like the way it sounds. It helps me fall asleep. MeMe says she's heard me say it in my sleep.

"MeMe, what does a Mommy do?" I ask. It has been so long since she died, I don't remember.

"Mommies do the same things as grandmothers," she said, "only faster."

At bedtime Mommy used to read me my favorite book and say prayers with me. Prayer was very important to her, and I miss hearing her voice. I miss snuggling with her. Now Daddy puts me to bed. He lays in bed with me and we talk about anything I want to talk about. I can ask him anything.

I ask him, "Daddy, will we be OK without Mommy?"

He hugs me close. "Yes, Peyton, we will," he said.

"How do you know?" I ask.

"Because it was important to Mommy that I promised her I would take care of us," he said. "I made a pinky promise to her that I would."

That makes me feel better. A pinky promise is a big deal in our family. Daddy would never break a pinky promise.

Daddy makes sure we do the things we loved to do as a family before Mommy got sick.

One of the things we still do is go to the high school games. Daddy is the football coach. Mommy loved to be in the stands every game. Now, Daddy has me for ballboy! I even get to ride the bus with the players and hang out with them before games. One time for fun, I raced across the football field so fast everyone was amazed!

"You could be an amazing football player someday," Daddy tells me. That makes me smile. I think Mommy would smile too.

Daddy still takes me to church every Sunday, because church was very important to Mommy. He still makes sure I have a great costume at Halloween. That was Mommy's favorite holiday. She used to enter me in the Halloween parade. I still have the first-place ribbons I won.

Daddy also makes sure that Christmas is still magical in our house. Mommy's birthday was just before Christmas. So Daddy gave me a special ornament to hang on the tree. The ornament is our way of making sure Mommy is still part of our Christmas.

Daddy makes sure the whole house is decorated inside and out. He even put a little tree in my room! I love having the tree to look at when I am in bed. It makes me feel closer to Mommy and the magic of Christmas.

Sometimes I worry I will forget her face or her voice. But MeMe assures me I won't. "After all, Peyton, you look just like her!" she says. "When you smile, I think of your Mommy."

That makes me feel better. I'm starting to smile more.

Today Daddy took me to do something special. He bought red balloons. We wrote messages on them to Mommy. We wrote things like "I miss you" and "I love you." We took the balloons to the cemetery and let them go. I watched them go up, up, up toward the sky. I hope Mommy got our messages.

I think Mommy got our messages. Tonight the big star in the sky twinkled at me. I think that was Mommy's way of telling me that everything will be all right. That makes me feel better.

Now that it's warmer outside, Daddy and I are going to do something very special for Mommy. We are putting together a race to raise money for other families. When I first heard the idea, I thought it was fantastic. Mommy loved to help other people.

Daddy says I can have a toy sale at the race. MeMe says she will help me put the sale together. My friends will help at the sale. We hope to raise lots of money for other families.

I am happy that so many people in our town brought toys to put in the sale. We had a lot of toys and a lot of shoppers. We raised a lot of money!

"Your mommy would be so proud of you," MeMe tells Daddy and me.

That makes me feel better.

I still miss Mommy. But I feel less sad. I know Mommy wishes she could be here with us. I know if she had a choice, she would not have gotten sick and left. I know she would want me to keep helping others the way she used to – and the way she probably is in Heaven.

Most of all, I know she loves me and Daddy very, very much. We will always love her and keep her locked in a special place in our hearts.

Twinkle, twinkle, Mother Star,

Look! I see you, there you are!

Far above the world so high,

Sending love across the sky.

Twinkle, twinkle, Mother Star,

Shining brightly from afar

The people behind the characters

Peyton Newell today
Peyton is now attending the University of Nebraska, where he plays football and maintains a 4.0 grade point average. He received 34 D-1 scholarship offers for football. He is active in community services and helps bring awareness to breast cancer. He loves life and realizes the importance of good friends and family.

Frank Newell (Daddy)
Frank accomplished every wish Missy (Mommy) asked of him for their son. He has worked very hard to help Peyton accomplish his dream. He has started over and is enjoying life again.

Judy Newell-Grandmother (MeMe)
Judy, a 12-year survivor of breast cancer, was integral in establishing Missys' Boutique at the University of Kansas Cancer Center, where she works daily with cancer patients to help give back what they feel they have lost.

Missy Newell (Mommy)
Missy passed away from breast cancer at age 32, when Peyton was 4. Frank and Peyton were her everything. The space she left in her loved ones' lives will never be filled, but they know they will see her again.

Special thanks to:

Howard Newell – A Loving Grandfather, Father and Father In Law

Stacie Newell - A Stepmom that was Meant to Be

Bradyn Newell - Peyton's #1 Fan and a Fantastic Little Brother

Sara Brunsvold - My guiding angel that helped make this book possible. I didn't know Sara until I looked for someone to help me thru the publication phase. I will always call her a friend and hope our paths will cross again.

Paul Howell - I was looking for an illustrator and by divine intervention our paths crossed. He is a generous friend with a big heart.

Marli Murphy - A friend and a loving volunteer at Missys' Boutique. I thank her for the poem that is so endearing.

Arlene Malter-Grandmother - Arlene gracefully built upon the Faith that Missy had already instilled in her son, Peyton.

Dale and Diane Wassergord – For their Passion and Continued Support to Missys' Boutique located at the University of Kansas Cancer Center. Also, to all of the people that have helped secure the legacy for " Two Missys" that lost their battle to Breast Cancer at a very young age. Missy Malter Newell and Missy Wilcox O'Neill.

Author's Note:

Sometimes we are so wrapped up in the disease we forget about the suffering of the caregiver. Our son, Frank, was there at every high and every low. A strong, loving husband and a loving father. A part of him died also with Missy. It took several years for him to be able to raise his head out of the sand. We as parents are very happy to see our son returning. He has remarried and has another son. I do believe Missy would approve, and she would have been crazy about Frank and Stacie's son Bradyn.

Peyton and Bradyn

Photo Credit: John S. Peterson, *Hail Varsity Magazine*

CPSIA information can be obtained
at www.ICGtesting.com
Printed in the USA
BVOW05*1133301017
499042BV00015B/206/P